TALES FROM THE HEN HOUSE

HOW THE SPECKLED HEN GOT HER SPECKLES AND OTHER STORIES

Edited by Charlotte Popescu

Published by Cavalier Paperbacks 2012

Cavalier Paperbacks
Burnham House,
Upavon,
Wilts SN9 6DU

www.cavalierpaperbacks.co.uk

ISBN 9781899470266

Printed and bound in Great Britain by
Jellyfish Print Solutions, Hollythorns House, New
Road, Swanmore, Hants SO32 2NW

Contents

HOW THE SPECKLED HEN GOT
HER SPECKLES
By Rhoda Power

Once upon a time there was a little white
hen. She had a pair of yellow claws and
feathers as white as milk. One day when
she was scratching in the ground she
found a scrap of paper.

"Tuk-a-tuk," said she, in great
surprise. "This must be a letter. Perhaps
the King dropped it when he passed this
way. I really must take it back to him."

She made herself tidy, put the little
bit of paper in a basket and set out for
the King's palace.

On the way she met a fox. Fortunately,
he was an old friend whom she had once
been able to help, so instead of

pouncing on her and eating her, he sat back on his hind legs and smiled.

"Where are you off to, little white hen?" asked he.

"Twork," clucked the hen. "I'm going to the palace to see the King. He's dropped a letter, which I've got in my basket."

"Oh indeed," said the fox. "May I come too?"

"Certainly! Certainly," clucked the hen. "I'll carry you in my basket."

So the fox made himself very small, squashed all his paws together and curled up in the basket and once again the little white hen set off on her journey. She had not gone very far before she came to a river.

"Good day, hen," said the river. "Why, aren't you the little white hen who did me such a great kindness last week by eating up the worms so that they shouldn't spoil my water?"

"Tawuk-tuk-tuk," answered the hen very modestly.

"Well, who'd have thought it!" said the river. "And where are you off to, may I ask?"

Twork-twork, said the hen, "I'm going to the King's palace. He dropped a letter.

I've got it in my basket."

"Really, said the river. "I do envy you. I've never seen the King. May I come too?"

"Certainly! Certainly! answered the hen. Curl up and get into the basket; but take care you don't drown Foxy. He's a friend of mine."

So the river curled itself round and round and round like cotton on a reel and rolled into the basket beside the fox and once again the little white hen set off on her journey. She could not go quite so quickly, because the basket was beginning to get heavy. However, she tottered along, until presently she came to a fire.

"Good day, hen," said the fire. "Why, surely you're the kind little white hen who fed me with dried grass when I was nearly out?"

"Tuk-tuk-tuk!" said the hen modestly.

The fire was delighted to see her again and crackled with pleasure.

"Pray where are you off to," it asked?

"Twork, twork, said the hen. "I'm going to the palace to speak to the King. He's dropped a letter. I've got it for him in my basket."

"You don't say so! Said the fire. "Well, if that isn't the biggest piece of luck that has ever come my way. I've never seen the King. Of course you'll take me with you, won't you?"

"Certainly! Certainly!" clucked the hen. "Get into the basket. But you must be very careful. Don't burn Foxy, and don't dry up the river. They're friends of mine!"

The fire flickered for a few minutes, but found that there was not enough room in the basket so it went out altogether, turned itself into ashes and crept into the basket beside the fox and the river.

Once again the little white hen set off on her journey, but she went very slowly, because the basket was extremely heavy and she did not reach the King's palace till next morning.

"Who's there?" asked the sentry when the little hen scratched at the door.

"Ta-tur-tuk! Ta-tur-tuk," cried the hen. "Please, sir, it's only me. A hen! I've found a letter which the King dropped. I've got it in my basket."

"Pass along, madam, if you please," said the sentry and so the hen went into

8

the courtyard and up to the door of the palace.

She felt very nervous but the fox and the river and the fire whispered to her through the wickerwork of the basket and she plucked up the courage, wiped her claws on the mat and walked in.

"Who's there?" asked the porter.

"Ta-tur-tuk! Ta-tur-tuk! Me, please!" said the hen. "I've found a letter which the King dropped. I've got it for him in my basket."

"This way, madam, if you please," said the porter and showed the hen into the throne room; and there was the King, with a crown on his head and a sceptre in his hand, surrounded by all the noble ladies and gentlemen of the Court.

The hen was in a nervous flutter. She had never been in such a grand palace before, and she hardly knew what to say. Luckily she did manage to remember her good manners. She slid one claw forward, one claw backward, spread out both her wings, and made a deep curtsey.

"Tuk-tuk-tuk-tarra-work!" said she, very gravely.

The King bowed. "Good day, hen!" said he, "and what may I do for you?"

"Tuk-tuk," answered the hen. "I've got a letter which Your Majesty dropped. I've brought it for you in my basket."

"A most intelligent bird!" said the King. "Bring forth the letter, hen!"

The hen put her basket on the floor and opened a tiny corner. She was afraid to show what else she had inside it, so she poked in her beak and brought out the little bit of paper, which she put in the King's hand.

But when the King saw the paper, his face grew purple with anger for one corner was wet and the other corner was burnt and in the middle there was a muddy mark where the fox had put his pad.

"Do you call that a letter?" he said. "You stupid bird! I'll eat you for dinner tomorrow!"

He stamped his foot and called for the servants. "Put that silly bird in the poultry yard," he said – "basket and all."

"Ta-work-tuk! Ta-work-tuk!" cried the hen in great distress. But it was no use. She was carried, squawking, from the palace and she and her basket were dropped into the poultry yard.

As you doubtless know, birds seldom like strangers and when the King's chickens saw the little white hen, they immediately flew at her and began to peck her. In the twinkling of an eye there was a bark of anger and out of the basket jumped the fox.

You should have seen the farmyard scatter! You should have heard the noise! Cluck, cluck! Quack, quack! Cock-a-doodle-do! The cows mooed, the donkeys brayed, the bulls bellowed, the horses neighed and the fox scattered all the King's cockerels and hens in every direction.

The noise reached the palace and out rushed the King and Queen, lord and lady, man and maid, shrieking, "Stop thief; stop thief. Catch that hen," and all went after the little white hen who ran as hard as she could with the basket in her beak.

It was awful for her, poor little thing. She ran and she ran till she could go no farther and then she fell down, just as the King had nearly caught her.

I said "nearly". He did not do it quite! Oh no! The river jumped out and splashed him, startling him so that he stopped short and when he looked up there was the river between him and the little white hen.

"Ho boatmen! Ho sailors! Row me across the river!" shouted the King but there were no boats.

"Ho swimmers, Ho divers! Tow me across," cried his Majesty, trembling with anger.

His obedient subjects leaped into the water and swam, pulling the King behind them and so before the poor little white hen had run very much farther, she found they were all after her again.

"Ta-work-tuk! Ta-work-tuk!" she cried, fluttering and running.

But they gained on her and they nearly caught her.

I said "nearly". They did not do it quite! Oh no! Just as the King stretched out his hand to grab her, the place grew dark and the King and the courtiers stood still, shouting, "Oo! Ow! There's dust or ashes or something in my eyes! I can't see a thing!"

On ran the little white hen. Oh wait a minute! Did I say white? She was not white any longer; she was speckled. Yes the ashes had jumped out of the basket so suddenly that she was covered with specks of ash.

Of course after that the King and his courtiers never found her. When they had rubbed the ashes out of their eyes, they searched high and low, but they could not find a white hen anywhere. They only saw a little specked hen, scratching by the roadside.

"Hi there," they cried. "Have you seen a white hen?"

"Ta-work-tuk-tuk!" cried the speckled hen wearily and went on scratching.

THE LITTLE GREY HEN
By Agnes Grozier Herbertson

There was once a little grey hen who lived at a hill farm. She had a nice wooden house in which to roost at night, a nice yard in which to run about by day and a nice green field in which to wander if she pleased, so she should have been quite happy.

But she wasn't, and I'll tell you the reason why. The trouble was that all the other hens were white and she alone was grey.

> It isn't in the least a joke
> With friends snow-white,
>   to be like smoke.

When visitors looked in at the farmyard they always said, "What lovely white hens!" And when they had looked about a little more they always cried, "Why there is one little grey hen. Dear me, what a pity."

Then the little grey hen felt dreadfully hurt. She rather hoped at first to wake up one morning and find that she was a little white hen, but this never happened.

She knew there was another farm about half way down the hill for she could see its chimneys. So one morning she set off to find a new home. For she thought the other farm might have quite a number of grey hens.

She travelled hopefully and hard
And soon she reached the new
farmyard.

So into the yard she went in a pleased kind of way.

She had not been there more than a few minutes when a fierce black cockerel flew out of the barn with a crow and a croak and a bustle.

"What? A grey hen!" he cried. "You don't belong here; out you go!"

And out the little grey hen went at top speed and in a terrible fright and made her way home.

So things went on as before.

Then one day a visitor said, "What, one little grey hen! I suppose she has strayed from the cottage at the foot of the hill. There are a number of grey hens there."

"No she isn't a stray, she belongs to me," the farmer's wife said in a not very pleased tone. "I shouldn't keep her if she didn't lay rather well."

The little grey hen had heard the visitor's remark. She had never been as far as the foot of the hill and didn't know anything about the cottage, but she decided at once to try her luck there. So on the very next day off she went.

The hill seemed very long indeed,
But down she went at a good speed,
Her feathers tidy and well kept,
As nice a hen as ever stepped.

Going along at that rate, she soon reached the cottage at the foot of the hill. It was a bright little cottage and to one side on a patch of green grass a number of little grey hens were roaming. In one corner was a neat hen house. But the most important thing was that all the hens but one were grey. The odd hen was a little white one but what did one white hen matter? So the little grey hen joined the other grey hens and you could see no difference except that the little grey hen had a green ring on one leg as had all the other hens at the farm.

Now the lady who lived at the cottage was not feeling very well so her daughter Susannah, fed the hens and fastened them up for the night in their nice hen house. She noticed at once the little grey hen with a green ring on her leg. "Oh what a lovely little hen!" she cried. "Where did you come from? Listen, you shall be my little hen because I found you here. And your name shall be Susie because my name is Susannah."

But when she told her mother she said, "She must have strayed from one of the farms; when I am better I must do something about it."

Two more days passed, and the little grey hen was very happy among the other grey hens, and she was kind to the little white hen remembering how lonely she had been.

But the lady of the cottage was better after two days and she came out to look at the hens. When she saw the green ring she said at once, "That little hen belongs to the farm on the hill. I must contact the farmer."

"Oh, Mummy, I can't bear to part with Susie," Susannah cried.

"I'm sorry but you can't keep a hen which belongs to somebody else," her mother said, and she phoned the farmer and his wife came the next day to fetch the little grey hen. "Yes, that's my hen. She is always straying," she said.

"I wonder if you would sell her to me," the lady asked, "for my little girl is very fond of her."

"The farmer's wife said she didn't want to sell her but she said, "I'll exchange her for that one white hen of yours for all my other hens are white."

Susannah's mother agreed to this and away went the little white hen. Susannah and Susie were delighted.

And now she had this pleasant home
She had no further wish to roam,
But lived, as happy as can be,
With other hens as grey as she.

MRS HEN'S BABIES
By Kenneth Harrow

The farmer brought four beautiful, big, white goose-eggs back from market and gave them to his wife. But she hadn't a goose to sit on them, so she gave them to an old speckled hen to look after.

The hen was a kind motherly old thing who sat on the eggs and kept them warm till one day: out came four little greeny yellow goslings. The first one surprised a wasp and a field mouse who were looking on. They wasted no time at all and began to nibble at the grass by their little house. Mrs Farmer gave them bread and milk too, but they preferred grass, and soon they had eaten all of it round their coop and it had to be moved into the field. The little geese had enormous great feet and funny little heads and bright eyes.

When they saw anything coming, they at once took up their strange goosey attitudes and tried to hiss like grown-up geese, but they could say only "Peep, peep!"

One day they found the pond. They did enjoy themselves in the mud and water and they ate a lot of watercress and almost any green leaves they could reach.

Mrs Hen didn't mind them going in the water; she had known the pond all her life and had often hunted for tadpoles at the edge, though of course she did not swim.

Like any other babies they soon got tired of walking and would sit down to graze.

Often they would creep under Mother's wing and have a nap. It was very cosy there, but they grew so fast that soon it was all Mrs Hen could do to cover them up. When she took them for a walk through the yard the other hens would stare after her rather rudely. They grew and they grew, till they were quite too big to be cuddled. They were very naughty and would peck at anything smaller than themselves.

There was a tub and a bucket where the bran mash was made for the calves, and the geese would help themselves from the bucket.

Sometimes one would climb on to the top of the old hen coop and looked as if he were talking to the others.

It seemed only a few weeks before most of the things in the yard were smaller than they were.

But if anything stood up to them and said "Boo!" they would run away squawking. Then old Mrs Hen would protect her wonderful babies, though they were much bigger than she was.

When the white goose spread her wings, she showed three pairs of little black feathers down her back, like buttons.

Two swans flew over one day and the geese were very excited and called after them but they did not come back.

Too big now to sleep in the hen coop, they were given a clean, empty pig-sty to sleep in. They had to be shut up at nights because there were foxes living near!

Every morning when they were let out they would make straight for the pond and dash into the water and frighten the farm ducks out in a hurry. Then they would stay and splash about and when they had washed they would stand on the bank and preen till every feather was spotless and perfect.

The summer grew very hot and dry so they were given a big basin of water in the yard. They gathered round it and pretended they were swimming and diving as they sat on the ground. Then it rained and the pond filled again and they dived under where the water was deep enough. They got more sensible as they grew older and one even made friends with the farm kittens and would nibble them gently but not hurt them.

One day when they were quite grown up one of them sat by the wall of the house and collected all the bits of straw and things it could reach and made a nest round itself as it sat there. Some days later when Mrs Farmer looked into the nest there were four beautiful, big white goose eggs! And then this story started all over again!

A LIMERICK By EDWARD LEAR

There was an old man with a beard
Who said, "It's just as I feared!
Two owls and a hen,
Four larks and a wren,
Have all built their nests in my beard!"

THE WANDERING CHICK
By Oscar Weigle

There was once a hen who had three chicks. The three chicks slept under her wing all night and hopped about the yard all day. At the end of the yard there was a big door that shut the world out. The chicks were too small to see the top of the door but they could peep underneath it by bending their necks.

The hen did not call her chicks by name, but by numbers. There was Number One, Number Two and Number Three. The Number One and Two were good, gentle, contented chicks that did not wish for more than they had got. But Number Three was not like them. He was tired of the yard and of seeing nothing but the things there and he wished to go into the world outside. At first he only began by wishing it a little and then went on to wish it a great deal till at last he wished it so much that he could not do without it. Instead of playing happily with his brothers on the steps in the yard, he went to the big door and stood looking at it and sighing. One afternoon his mother found him there.

"What do you want?" she asked.

"I want to get out," answered the chick.

"Why?" said his mother.

"I don't know," answered the chick, "but I want to get out."

The hen shook her head. "You're far better off at home," she said. "It's no use wishing for it. Go and play on the steps with your brothers."

The chick did so because he had to obey. He tried to play happily like the others but all the while he was thinking of the big door and the world that lay outside.

When it was time for bed under the hen's wing, he scarcely slept for thinking of it. If he slept at all, it was only to dream that he had left.

This went on for a week. After a week he could bear it no longer.

"Today," he said, "When Mother is sleeping and Number One and Number Two are round the corner of the hen house, I'll squeeze under the door and get out."

He did not tell this to anybody. After breakfast he played with the others as usual. At last, his mother hung her head and shut her eyes and Number One and Number Two went to play beside the hen house. The time had come. The chick ran to the big door very softly, looked round the yard with a beating heart, squeezed himself under it and with a hard tug to get through, stood upright in the world outside. Oh it was very delicious! The air of the world was so fresh and there was so much of it and there was no end to the things he saw for at every step he saw something new.

"This is much nicer than the yard," said the chick drawing himself up.

"This is really living!"

He walked along looking about him. "It's not only wider," said he, "but higher. I'm sure it's higher than the yard. I can't see the top of it."

Presently he met an animal standing under a tree. He did not know its name, for he had never seen one like it before in his life.

"Oh big animal," said the chick, boldly, "Have you been in the world long?"

"Oh yes little chick!" said the animal.

"I've only just come in," said the chick, "and I like it very much. There's so much room."

"Room enough for you, certainly," said the animal. "Where are you going?"

"How can you ask me," said the chick, "When I tell you I've just come in?"

"I'll tell you then," said the animal. "Go back home. Don't go any farther."

"Everyone tells me that," said the chick. "But I shan't. Our yard is so narrow – I can't stay in it."

"I advise you," said the animal, "to run back home. I'm not only bigger than you, but wiser."

The chick went on without minding him.

"Either I am very small or some things are very big," he thought. While he looked around him, he forgot about the yard and his mother and Number One and Number Two. The day passed without his noticing it.

"I shan't be able to see much longer," said the chick.

"It's getting dark. I must ask for something to eat. I feel terribly hungry."

He was standing in the grass where a great many creatures lived.

"Mr Snail," said the chick. "I'm hungry. Give me something to eat."

"I have nothing to give you," answered the snail. "It's not my business."

"But I'm hungry," said the chick feeling very uncomfortable.

But the snail was gone.

The chick walked on. He felt almost too hungry to look about him. Presently he saw a bird.

"Mr Bird," he said. "I'm hungry. Give me something to eat."

The bird stared. "Why," he said, "you don't belong to me. It's not my business." And he flew away.

The chick went on. The darkness was coming on.

"How black it does get in the world!" said the little thing, shivering. "And how very cold it is with nothing at all to warm one!"

He stood still as he was too tired to walk on. Besides he had lost his way in the world.

Presently a field mouse peeped out at him.

"I'm hungry!" called the chick. "Do give me something to eat."

"Find something for yourself," said the field mouse. "It's not my business."

The poor little chick now hung its head. "The world must be very empty," he said, with a sigh, "if they can't spare me something out of it. I should have thought there would have been more than enough for everybody but I suppose it's smaller than I thought."

Presently a grasshopper came up.

"I'm so hungry!" said the chick. "Do give me something to eat."

"You must feed yourself, chick," said the grasshopper. "I've got enough to feed at home. It isn't my business."

"I'll not ask any more," thought the poor little chick, "for it's no use. I wish I was back in the yard. The world may be very big and grand to look at, but it's very uncomfortable to live in." And he hung his head again. He was so tired.

Suddenly he felt himself lifted up in the air. He opened his eyes and saw a man. He had seen two men in his life before.

"I'm so hungry!" said the chick, though he did not expect anything to come of it. "Will you give me something to eat?"

The man held him close in his warm hand, without answering and the chick stopped shivering.

"I shall soon be too hungry to speak!" he thought.

They moved on silently. The chick grew weaker and weaker. "I shall soon be too hungry to live," he thought.

At last the man stopped at the door out of the world. The man opened it and went in. Then he bent down and put the chick down gently on the ground and there stood his mother.

"Mother," said the chick. "There's nothing to eat outside in the world. Do give me something!"

The hen did so in a great hurry. She was delighted to see him.

"Number Three," she said, when he had quite finished, "Come under my wing and rest. You must be very tired."

"Very," said the little chick, creeping in. "How nice and warm it is here! It was so dreadfully cold outside! Good night, Mother."

And Number Three fell asleep and never woke till the sun rose in the morning.

THE COCKEREL AND THE CENTIPEDE
A Chinese Fairy Story

When the Jasper Emperor still ruled the heavens, the cockerel did not look as he does today. On his head he had beautiful antlers like a stag's and he was very proud of them. All the beasts envied him these antlers, especially the dragon who lived in a deep pool. The dragon had a head shaped like a camel's, eyes like the devil's, ears like a buffalo's, a neck like a snake's, talons like a vulture's and pads like a tiger's. What made him unhappy was the fact that his camel-shaped head was quite bald.

One day the Jasper Emperor invited all the animals to a banquet at the Celestial Palace. All the animals looked forward to this banquet. Only the dragon was unhappy. He wondered how he could cover his bald head. He was still wondering when the cockerel came strutting past the dragon's pool. He carried himself like a lord and on his head were his beautiful antlers.

The dragon said to him, "Tomorrow, Cockerel, I am invited to the Celestial Palace to the banquet and I have nothing to wear on my head. Will you lend me your antlers?"

"I cannot, Dragon," replied the cockerel. "I too am invited to the Celestial Palace."

"But even without your antlers you look quite handsome," the dragon said in a flattering way. "You have such beautiful feathers, a splendid tail and such fine spurs. I would even say those antlers detract from your beauty!"

At that moment the centipede went past. When she heard what the dragon said, she immediately joined in the conversation.

"The dragon is quite right, Brother

Cockerel," she said. "You are beautiful even without these antlers. Take my advice and lend them to the dragon. If you like, I shall guarantee their safety."

And so, in the end the cockerel allowed himself to be persuaded.

"I shall lend them to you for one day, Dragon," he promised. "After the banquet you must give them back to me."

The dragon promised to return the antlers immediately after the banquet. Happily he put them on his head and set out for the Celestial Palace.

Then Jasper Emperor welcomed all the animals and asked them to be seated. The dragon he placed next to himself. The cockerel was annoyed.

"It is because I lent my antlers to the dragon," he complained.

Next day he went to the pool. "Dragon," he called, "give me back my antlers!" But the dragon had forgotten his promise. He liked the antlers and had no intention of giving them back.

"What use are they to you, Brother Cockerel?" he said. "You are good looking enough without them, while I must have something on my head."

The cockerel was angry. "It is my business whether I am good looking or not," he said. "Give me back what you borrowed!"

The dragon took no notice of the cockerel's cry. "Don't be angry, Brother Cockerel. I have other things to do than argue with you. We shall talk about it another time," he said and dived, with the antlers, to the bottom of the pool.

The cockerel set up a cry. "Dragon, give me back my antlers! Dragon, give me back my antlers!"

But he cried in vain. The dragon at the bottom of the pool, could not hear him. But the centipede heard him and she came running to ask what was happening.

"The dragon will not give me back my antlers," cried the cockerel. "And you are a witness to his promise."

"That is true," said the centipede, "but what can I do when the dragon has gone into hiding at the bottom of the pool?"

"What's that to me?" he said. "You should not have guaranteed for him."

The centipede snapped back. "And you should not have lent him your antlers. It is all your own fault."

The cockerel was beside himself. "It's your fault!" he shrieked, opened his beak, pecked at the centipede and pecked her right in half.

Ever since then, the cockerel and the centipede have been enemies. A cockerel has only to catch sight of a centipede and he is after it at once to kill it and eat it. And the cockerel has not forgotten the dragon, either. When he wakes up in the morning he shouts, "Cockadoodle-doo!" which in cockerel language means, "Dragon, give me back my antlers!"

But to this day the dragon has not given them back, as you can see for yourselves.

COCKLE BUTTON, COCKLE BEN
The Story of two Plymouth Rocks
By Richard Phibbs

Bobbie Shaftoe has a hen,
Cockle Button, Cockle Ben,
She lays eggs for gentlemen,
But none for Bobbie Shaftoe

Cockle Button was a Plymouth Rock, plump and comfortable and speckled grey. And Cockle Ben was a Plymouth Rock with a fine red comb and a pair of spurs, and he was a speckled grey too. They lived together at The Old Parsonage Farm. In the daytime they pecked about the barnyard quite happily with the other hens but at night they roosted alone together in the orchard, on a big leaning apple tree.

"I find the roosting shed too hot," said Cockle Button and they only used it in wet weather. The other hens were not offended.

Cockle Button was not a good layer but the farmer's wife was very proud of her and Cockle Ben and thought she would like to show them at the May Fair in the market town. So the farmer got a big roll of wire-netting and some posts and went out into Alice O'Hara's field at the end of the garden. There he drove the posts into the ground. Then he fixed the wire-netting round them with staples and made a pen. But between the two last posts he left a space for the hen house. The house had little iron wheels and hooks at each side to fix it to rings in the posts. The farmer's wife caught Cockle Ben and Cockle Button and put them into the hen house through the roof which had hinges. Cockle Ben and Cockle Button walked straight out of the hen house through the front door.

"Let us return to the orchard," said Cockle Button. And she ran across the grass hill till she came to the wire-netting. And Cockle Ben ran too.

"We will walk along this fence and squeeze out under the gate," said Cockle Ben. They walked right round the pen.

"We have missed the way out," said Cockle Button. She started round again uneasily, muttering to herself. Cockle Ben went round in the opposite direction and they met outside the hen house and went in and sat down together to consider.

"I see no way out," said Cockle Ben, "I think the woman will return shortly with an explanation."

"I see no way out," said Cockle Button, "and I think the woman will return shortly with a knife."

"I remember the turkeys," said Cockle Ben, beginning to fidget.

"It's a trap, I know it's a trap! Oh my dear! A trap to boil us." Cockle Button ran out of the house and flew screaming round the pen. Cockle Ben ran too. He was very much upset by the remarks of Cockle Button. He tried to fly out of the pen and over the wire, but the wire was too high and he only flew against it.

They were both dishevelled and quite tired out when the farmer's wife brought them their supper. Before she could get inside the pen she had to move the hen house. It was beginning to rain and she put the food down quickly and went out again and gave the house a good hard push back into place. Then she ran indoors. Cockle Button and Cockle Ben ate their supper and went in out of the wet too. And in spite of the rain on the roof they soon went to sleep. Next morning they forgot they had been frightened and went out in the sunshine to dig for worms. The ground was soft after the rain and the grass had been cropped short by Alice O'Hara, the cow.

Cockle Ben saw Alice O'Hara and the farmer coming back to the field from the milking shed and he crowed very loudly. Alice came across the field to the pen and the farmer shut the gate and went to the vegetable garden to plant potatoes. Alice came up quite close to the wire and looked through. Cockle Ben wished her good morning and went on digging. But Cockle Button did not say anything. She had just remembered that she wasn't in the orchard. She was just beginning to remember what had happened yesterday. Then she noticed Alice. Alice had a black and white face but a very soothing expression. Cockle Button ran across the pen and began explaining everything. When Cockle Ben heard Cockle Button talking to Alice he began to remember yesterday and told Alice about it too. With the two of them talking at once, Alice was muddled. She didn't answer but just went round the back of the hen house and began to scratch herself against it. Cockle Button and Cockle Ben ran up to the wire beside the hen house and politely asked Alice to advise them about their escape but Alice didn't take any notice, even when they shouted at her. She just had a good long scratch and then went away grazing.

Cockle Ben and Cockle Button were in despair. They did not cheer up even when Jenny, the farmer's daughter, threw their morning grain in through the wire. Cockle Button took a few pecks of grain and wandered off sadly round the pen. Suddenly she saw the way out.

Now this is what had happened. When the farmer's wife had brought Cockle Button and Cockle Ben their supper, she had not stopped to hook the hen house to the rings. So there was the hen house, just wedged between the posts. And when Alice was having her good long scratch, she had pushed it a little and a little more till it was sticking out half inside the pen.

So what did Cockle Button do? She ran and she jumped and she flapped her wings and she flew up on top of the hen house. And she was just going to fly out over the top of the wire, when she remembered Cockle Ben. So she flew down to fetch him and showed him the hen house sticking out into the pen. And when he saw it he spread his wings and flew up on to the roof and spread his wings again and flew right over the wire and landed in the field.

But Cockle Button was still inside the pen. Cockle Ben called to her to hurry. She tried to fly up on to the roof of the hen house, but she was so flustered and excited that she fell back three times before she managed it. When she did get on to the roof she sat down to have a little rest, but Cockle Ben kept running up and down outside and flustered her. So she stood up on the roof and flapped once and twice and flew up towards the top of the wire but she didn't fly over the top, she just hit the top instead and fell back right down in front of the hen house, all shaken up and untidy. Cockle Ben went on talking very loudly from beyond the wire, but Cockle Button didn't hear him. She just walked around in a little circle and sat down feeling dizzy.

"I will have a little drink of water and go to bed. I ache," said Cockle Button. But just as she was going to get her little drink of water, Cockle Ben shouted out that he could see the farmer coming down the garden path, that he could see the farmer opening the gate, that he could see the farmer beginning to run across the field ... And Cockle Ben didn't wait any longer. He just ran across the field towards the hedge, through the hedge and into Hangar Wood beyond. And when Cockle Button saw what was happening she forgot that she was dizzy and she flew very easily up on to the hen house roof and she flapped and she flapped and she flew right out over the wire into the field and ran after Cockle Ben – but the farmer ran too. And he was just going to catch Cockle Button, when he stumbled over a mole hill and down he fell flat on his face. When he got up there was no sign of Cockle Button and no sight of Cockle Ben either. This annoyed the farmer and he went along by the ditch, beating the hedge with his spade. But he soon got tired of that. "They will come in at supper time," he said and went back to the garden.

When the farmer had gone, Cockle Button came out of the wet ditch and called Cockle Ben. Cockle Ben flew down out of a holly bush. He looked ashamed but Cockle Button did not scold him.

Alice O'Hara had not seen Cockle Ben and Cockle Button fly over the wire; she had been occupied grazing at the other side of the field but she had seen them running to the wood with the farmer after them. She walked over to them when they came out of the hedge.

"We just flew out over the wire," said Cockle Ben, "there was no difficulty." Alice looked at the pen then she looked at Cockle Button rearranging her feathers, then she went and walked round the pen and came back to the hedge.

"Well, it's you that has agility," said Alice O'Hara. Then she went on grazing and couldn't advise them what to do next.

Cockle Ben and Cockle Button went back into the wood, for fear they might be seen if they stayed there talking to Alice. They went right through the wood to the main road. Drawn up by the side of the road was a car and on the bank the people were having a picnic. They threw crumbs of cake and Cockle Button and Cockle Ben gladly picked them up. Then the people left their car and went off for a walk. Cockle Button and Cockle Ben went close to the car and were picking up the rest of the crumbs, when they heard the noise of a horse and cart along the road. They looked out from behind the car and saw the farmer's boy driving back from the woodman's cottage. Cockle Ben and Cockle Button jumped hastily into the boot and hid under some sacking. They were just thinking of coming out when the people came back. The hamper was packed and the boot shut. The people got in and drove the car off. Cockle Button and Cockle Ben went to sleep. They woke again when the car stopped. The people got out, a man opened the boot and took out the hamper. Cockle Ben and Cockle Button were discovered. They were too sleepy to run away.

The chauffeur picked them up and shut them in a wood shed and went to tell the cook. Cockle Ben flew up to roost on the rafters. Cockle Button made a nest in the saw dust. She couldn't remember when she'd laid her last egg. Of course she made a great fuss about it and Cockle Ben flew down to look at it and they made so much noise that the chauffeur looked in, saw the egg and took it to the cook who told the gentlemen who were pleased.

But Cockle Ben and Cockle Button were left in the wood shed. Nobody remembered to feed them and by morning they were faint with hunger. Cockle Button laid again, but the egg had a soft shell.

After breakfast the cook asked the butler what to do with the two chickens in the wood shed and the butler went to ask the gentleman who said, "We must return them this morning to the farmer. We can land at Denbury on our way to the regatta and a van can take them home." The gentleman had nine horses, three cars, an aeroplane and nothing much to do.

So Cockle Button and Cockle Ben were packed in an uncomfortably small hamper and flown away in an aeroplane. At Denbury a van took them to the farm. When the farmer's wife unpacked them they were very stiff and hungry. They don't look good for much now," said the farmer's wife. And she fed Cockle Ben and Cockle Button and turned them into the orchard.

Next morning Cockle Ben called across to Alice in the meadow. "Where have you been all this time?" said Alice.

"We went away by car to see the world," said Cockle Ben.

"And did the same car bring you back again?" said Alice.

And Cockle Ben stood up in the leaning apple tree and flapped his wings and crowed. "Oh there was no difficulty about getting back," said Cockle Ben, "We flew."

Alice had seen the van from Denbury and she looked at Cockle Ben preening in the morning: "Well it's you that has agility!" said Alice.

THE BROWNY HEN
by Irene F Fawsey

A browny hen sat on her nest
With a hey-ho for the springtime!
Seven brown eggs 'neath her downy breast,
With a hey-ho for the springtime!

A brown hen clucks all day from dawn,
With a hey-ho for the springtime!
She's seven wee chicks as yellow as corn,
With a hey-ho for the springtime!

THE CROCODILE AND THE HEN
A Fairy Story from Africa

Once upon a time a hen came to the river to drink. A hungry crocodile saw her and thought what a nice, plump hen she was.

"I shall have a good dinner," said the crocodile happily and grabbed the hen by the tail. But the hen began to shriek. "Let me go, Crocodile, let me go, dear brother!"

The crocodile was amazed. "Why does the hen call me brother," he wondered? And he let her go.

The next day the hen came to the river again. The hungry crocodile was waiting for her and grabbed her by the wing. But again the hen let out a great shriek. "Let me go, Crocodile, let me go, dear brother."

Unwillingly the crocodile let her go. But after all he was not going to eat his sister. He kept turning the matter over in his mind, however, and at last he went to his friend the lizard for advice.

"Listen to what happened to me, Lizard," he said. "I caught a hen by the river, but when I wanted to eat her she started shrieking that I should let her go and she called me her dear brother. Am I the brother of a hen?"

The lizard began to laugh. "The hen was telling the truth, Crocodile. Don't you know that hens are hatched out of eggs, just as crocodiles are?"

The crocodile nodded. "You are quite right, Lizard, I had never thought about it before. If you look at it that way the hen really is my sister, or at least my niece."

And ever afterwards the crocodile left hens in peace.

SPECKLED EGGS
By Margaret Baker

There was once a black hen who laid brown, speckled eggs. All the other hens in the farmyard laid eggs with plain white shells and so the black hen was very proud of herself.

"When I have eleven eggs I will sit on them and hatch out a family," she used to boast, "They will be exceptionally fine chicks because they will be hatched from exceptionally fine eggs!"

But the black hen never had eleven eggs. She would spend half the morning looking for a quiet and secret spot for her nest, but her trouble was always wasted because as soon as she had laid an egg she began to cackle.

"It's a speck-eck-eck-eck-eckled one! It's a speck-eck-eck-eck-eckled one!" she would call at the top of her voice and then, of course, Susan the dairymaid, or Mrs Clutterbrook, the farmer's wife would run to the door or the window to see from which direction the black hen was coming so that they would know where to look for the egg.

The hen made a point of going round the farmyard to tell the news. She went into the cow-house and the stable and the barn and past the pig-sties and the kennel and the pump to the duck-pond and all the way she cackled loudly, "It's a speck-eck-eck-eck-eckled one! It's a speck-eck-eck-eck-eckled one!"

"All that fuss for an egg," grunted the pigs; "now if she had found the gate open into the turnip field there would be some reason for making a noise!"

But just as surely as the black hen went cackling proudly round the farmyard in the morning, she spent the afternoon wandering up and down complaining. "It's g—one," she would wail! "it's g—one! It isn't fair!"

"Can't have you going on like this every day," said Towser, the sheep dog, who acted as policeman.

"It's all very well to say that," cried the black hen excitedly, "but somebody steals my eggs every dinner-time and they're very special ones – they're brown and speckled!"

"It doesn't matter if they're striped," said Towser, "we can't have the whole place upset like this. First you go round shouting that you've laid an egg and then you go round moaning that it's stolen; there's no peace at all and I've had a lot of complaints."

"Complaints," cried the black hen; "how very unkind! But I know what it is, you're all jealous of me! If you were clever enough to lay speckled eggs you'd cackle yourself!"

"That's just where you're wrong, ma'am," said Towser; "when I've something I don't want stolen I take care to keep quiet about it, that beef bone, for instance – but there now, I'm telling … Take my advice, ma'am and next time you've an egg you want to keep for yourself…"

"I always want to keep my eggs for myself," interrupted the hen; "I've been trying for weeks to collect eleven to make a sitting."

"Then take my advice," repeated Towser; "don't make a single cackle! Keep quiet! Then, don't you see, everyone will be satisfied; you'll have your eggs, the rest of the farmyard will have a little peace and it will be happy all round."

"A little peace indeed," clucked the hen and stalked away, but all the same she thought Towser's idea was a good one and determined to try it.

She spent the rest of the afternoon poking her beak into every hole and corner in the farmyard and orchard; she was so busy that she almost overlooked feeding time but in the end she found the perfect place for a nest. It was among a tangle of nettles and brambles at the back of the dairy and the joke of it was that it was so close to the dairy window that no one would ever think of looking for her there.

Next morning the black hen strolled into the orchard as though by accident; she scratched a little under the trees and chased a stray moth and then when she was sure no one was looking, she slipped under the brambles. The ducks waddled past on their way to the pond, the pigs snuffled about within a few steps of her and she heard Susan in the dairy, but not one of them discovered her hiding place.

"It's a speck-eck ..." she began from habit as she crept out of the brambles and then remembered just in time. She looked anxiously to right and left but fortunately no one was near.

"I must remember not to cackle. I must remember not to cackle," she kept saying and only a hen could know how difficult it was to keep quiet.

The geese were preening themselves near the pump.

"It's a speck ..." she began again and then stopped and pretended to be very busy wiping her beak on a stone.

"What did you say," said the gander.

"Oh, nothing important," said the black hen hastily; "a little dust got into my throat and made me cough."

She hurried away for fear she should forget again. Half a dozen times as she went round the yard she had to choke back a cackle and at last she took a walk along the lane to the cow field because she was not likely to meet anyone and so there would be no temptation to talk.

When she came back she went to peep at the nest under the brambles; the egg was still there!

For the rest of the day the black hen strutted about the yard with her head held so high that she passed a handful of corn and a very fat caterpillar without seeing them.

"Feeling mighty pleased with yourself today, aren't you," said the turkey?

The black hen hurried on without replying; she did not dare to open her beak, for she was sure that if she did she would cackle, "It's a speck-eck-eck-eck-eckled one!" Before she could stop herself.

Every morning after that she wandered into the orchard trying to look as if she had not a thought in her mind but the chance of pecking up a slug or two and when she was sure no one was looking she slipped on to her nest and laid an egg. She still wanted to rush back to the farmyard cackling loudly for all the world to hear but she found a walk to the cow field calmed her down.

"The farm's a different place since that black hen stopped laying," grunted the pigs as they settled down for their afternoon nap.

The hen overheard them. "Stopped laying, indeed!" she thought to herself and poked her head into a pile of straw for fear anyone should notice her amusement.

Day by day the number of eggs under the brambles increased and at last there were ten.

"I shall only have to lay one more," said the hen; "eleven is the ideal size for a family. I shall take particular care to train the chicks well. 'My dears,' I will say as I gather them under my wings, 'remember that whatever happens you must never cackle; if I had cackled you would not be here now'."

Next morning as usual she sauntered into the orchard and crept on to her nest.

"The black hen's keeping very quiet lately," grunted the pigs as they dug for roots near the brambles.

"All cackle, that's what it was," said the turkey; "I don't believe she ever laid a speckled egg in her life!"

"Oh haven't I," thought the hen? "And here am I sitting on eleven of the finest and brownest and most speckled ones you could find!"

Mrs Clutterbrook came into the dairy to help Susan skim the milk. "That black hen's downright lazy," she said crossly; "she's not laid an egg for a fortnight and the vicar's wife specially asks for them; she says the vicar likes one for his breakfast."

"Oh indeed," the hen chuckled to herself; "then I'm afraid he'll have to be satisfied with plain white ones in future."

The ducks waddled past the brambles in a long line. "Do you remember the fuss that used to be made of that black hen," asked one?

"I did hear she wanted to get eleven eggs and hatch a family," said another, "but she couldn't do it, she cackled too much."

"Quack, quack, quack," they all laughed; "to think of her keeping quiet long enough to collect a sitting of eggs! All hens are stupid, but she was the stupidest in all the farmyard. Quack, quack, quack!"

That was more than the black hen could stand. She scrambled off her nest. "I'm stupid, am I?" she cackled loudly; "that's all you know about it! I've laid the last of the eleven eggs this morning and they're all speck-eck-eckled! They're very speck-eck-eck-eck-eckled!

Up flew the dairy window and out popped Susan's head.

"Oh Mrs Clutterbrook, ma'am, I do believe the black hen's been and made a nest under our very noses," she screamed. "There must be dozens of eggs in it!"

Too late the black hen saw what she had done. She had cackled! Now all the eggs would disappear at once and she would never have a family. She stretched her neck and spread her wings and rushed shrieking round and round the orchard and into the farmyard.

Mrs Clutterbrook clapped her hands over her ears. "For goodness' sake, Susan, shut that window and leave the nest alone!" She shouted above the noise; "there'll be no living within a mile of that hen unless we let her sit!"

So, after all, the eleven eggs were allowed to hatch into eleven chicks and if they were not quite the finest chicks in all the world, their mother thought they were and that is nearly the same thing. She brought them up very carefully; she taught them how to catch grasshoppers and scratch for worms and preen their feathers and they all grew up into black hens and laid brown speckled eggs. They had just one fault – it was a fault their mother had before them – they could not help cackling.

THREE LITTLE CHICKENS

Said the first little chicken
With a queer little squirm,
"Oh I wish I could find
A fat little worm!"

Said the second little chicken
With a small sigh of grief,
"Oh I wish I could find
A little green leaf!"

Said the third little chicken
With a sharp little squeal,
"Oh I wish I could find
Some nice yellow meal!"

"Now see here," said their mother
From the green garden patch,
"If you want any breakfast
You must all come and scratch!"

MR FOX AND THE BANTAMS
By Christine Pullein-Thompson

Tommy was a very proud bantam cockerel. He had long shiny feathers and speckled legs with spurs on them. As soon as it was light each day he crowed: "I am the best and bravest cockerel in the world."

Tommy had four wives – Cowslip, Spice, Nutty and Daisy. Cowslip and Nutty always obeyed Tommy. Spice flattered him. Only Daisy argued with him, saying things like, "Why should I?" and "I don't want to," which annoyed him no end. It was because of this that Tommy often pecked Daisy so hard that her comb bled and then he would shout, "It's all your own fault. I am master of the hen run." But Daisy who was very obstinate just went on arguing. One evening, the humans, whom the bantams called, 'the people' were late shutting the bantams in their house for the night. It grew darker and darker and then a lovely moon appeared. By this time Tommy had told his wives that they were to sleep on the roof of their house for the night. "One two, one two," he crowed and gave Daisy a hasty peck to make her hurry. Soon Tommy was sitting between his four wives, feeling very proud. I really am master of the hen run, he thought before falling into a deep, happy sleep.

It was Daisy who first heard Mr Fox digging beneath the wire netting which surrounded their run. For a moment she was too frightened to move.

"Five juicy bantams for dinner tonight," Mr Fox was saying to himself, his mouth watering, his eyes bright with greed. "Yum, yum."

Then Daisy started to squawk. "Help, help. Mr Fox is here," and she flew off the top of the house flapping her wings in terror. Another second and all the bantams were flying around the run trying to get out, but they were trapped because the people had clipped their wings and they could only fly a metre in the air and the wire netting around their run was three metres high.

Tommy tried to be brave. "I will see off Mr Fox," he crowed, his heart, thumping wildly in his small body.

But the bantams all knew that no one could defeat Mr Fox. He was too big and his teeth were too sharp.

Mr Fox was under the wire now; another second and he had grabbed poor Tommy in his strong jaws. "Help, he's killing me," screeched Tommy.

"Help, help," squawked Daisy, Nutty, Spice and Cowslip. Luckily at that very moment the people arrived home. Hearing the commotion, they ran to the hen run shouting to one another.

"It's the fox. He's killing the bantams."

But faster than them ran their dog, Bob. When Mr Fox saw Bob, he dropped

Tommy and ran away faster than he had ever run before.

The people picked up poor Tommy who was gasping and gasping in a terrible way. "I'll take him up to the house and give him a drop of brandy," said the woman who was called Mrs Judd.

The man, Mr Judd, gently shooed Nutty, Spice, Cowslip and Daisy into the hen house and shut the door. Then he called Bob, who was looking very important, and went away.

The hens felt lonely without Tommy, even Daisy missed him a little bit. The next day the people put an electric fence around the outside of the run to keep Mr Fox away. Then they brought back Tommy who looked quite different now. He couldn't walk straight any more (which might have been caused by the brandy) and he had lost all his beautiful feathers, which made him look much, much smaller. The hens were too shocked to say anything. It was a long time before Tommy crowed again and when he did, he crowed, "Wake up, wake up, it's a lovely morning," instead of, "I am the best cockerel in the world."

Cowslip, Nutty and Spice felt sorry for Tommy. But Daisy was happy because he didn't peck her any more.

Gradually Tommy's feathers came back, just as long and silvery as before. But he had changed, though he now looked the same. He didn't say, "I'm master of the hen run," ever again. He was really polite to his wives; sometimes even saying, "I'm sorry," and when in the Spring Daisy's eggs hatched five chicks Tommy was a perfect father. As for Mr Fox he was never ever seen again.

PATTY HEN
By Gregor Ian Smith

Patricia was a little white hen. She lived with her ten sisters in the big brown hen house at Strawberry Farm. Patricia had always been a bit of a problem right from the day she was hatched. She had always been smaller, and slimmer and very much quieter than any of the others. In this way she gave everyone the impression of being rather a delicate pullet.

Before Patricia was very old, she realised that something would have to be done about her name. "Patricia" was much too big a name for a small hen. Everyone laughed when they heard it. And so, rather than have all this fuss and giggling every time her name was mentioned, she decided to shorten it to "Patty", which you will agree was much better.

Now Patty had one complaint. She suffered from cold feet. It wasn't so bad in summer when the weather was fair and warm, but in winter when the puddles were frozen over, and frost and snow powdered the ground, Patty was most uncomfortable. This was bad enough during the day, but during the long, dark nights the chill that spread from toes to ankles was so bad she simply could not get a wink of sleep.

"It just can't go on," she told herself one night, as she looked around the sleeping hens on the perch. "I must get to sleep, too!"

"What's that, Patty," said the sleepy voice of Diana Duck?

"My feet are so cold I can't get to sleep," replied the little white hen.

"No wonder. Why you should want to sit up there on a draughty perch, I can't understand! Cuddle down as I do, in a corner, and fluff out your feathers. Then you'll soon fall asleep."

Patty took Diana's advice. But when she tried sleeping on the floor, the draughts seemed worse than ever.

Malcolm Mouse peeped in. "Try curling up in a ball, Patty as I do," he suggested. "It's the only sensible way to sleep. And if you don't believe me, ask the rats, and the rabbits, and the dogs and the cats and the lambs. They all curl up before they sleep."

Patty lay down again with a sigh. She tried to curl up and make her tail and her beak touch, but of course, it was quite impossible. All she succeeded in doing was to wake up the other hens.

"Look!" they cried, in astonishment, "Patty Hen has fainted!" But when she explained to them that she was only trying to sleep, they were very angry with her for disturbing them. Poor Patty had to climb back to her perch again, more miserable than ever.

Then suddenly she remembered old Mr Owl. He lived in the barn, and he was so wise he knew everything - or nearly everything. Patty wondered if he knew how to cure cold feet, and if he could help her to get to sleep.

In the morning she hurried off to the barn. Mr Owl was in his favourite corner looking very wise.

"Please Mr Owl," said Patty, trying not to yawn, "Will you help me?"

Mr Owl nodded his head solemnly and listened while she told him her troubles.

"Dearie me, Patty Hen," he replied. "Give me half an hour to think it over, then perhaps I'll be able to help."

Patty Hen went off for half an hour. When she returned, Mr Owl had thought of a plan.

"Now my dear, you must pay attention. First of all you must visit Christabel the cow. Tell her your troubles and I'm quite sure she'll let you sleep on one of her horns."

"Oh dear," thought Patty! "I've never slept on a cow's horn before. But thank you, Mr Owl I'll try."

Christabel the cow was surprised when Patty Hen paid her a visit that afternoon. Patty was afraid at first, for Christabel was a large cow, with long horns and a loud voice.

"Excuse me, Christabel," Patty began timidly. "Mr Owl said you might be able to help me. I can't get to sleep because my feet are cold. Mr Owl thought that you might let me sleep on one of your horns."

Christabel looked at the sad little hen, then smiled. "Now isn't that strange! I find it very hard to sleep too, because my left ear tickles. If I allowed you to sleep on my horn, Patty, do you think you could give my ear a little peck now and again to stop it tickling?"

"Oh yes, indeed," replied Patty. "I'll peck it any time you ask. Thank you very much."

"Very well," agreed the old cow. "Off you go. But you must come to bed soon after supper, for I must be up early in the morning."

That evening after supper, Patty hurried to the byre where Christabel was waiting. She lowered her head gently, and Patty hopped on to one of her horns. To the little hen's surprise, it was both smooth and warm.

"Now if you please, Patty, just one little peck before you go off to sleep," said the cow.

Patty pecked the ear that tickled. Christabel said "Thank you," and they both settled down for the night. Very soon, Patty was so warm and comfortable she fell sound asleep.

Patty Hen still sleeps in the byre at Strawberry Farm; and thanks to Christabel, she sleeps the whole night through, because her feet are always warm as pies. As for Christabel, she is the most contented cow alive, for her left ear doesn't tickle any more.

THE FOX AND THE COCKEREL
From Aesop's Fables

All though the history of the world no animals have done such clever things as the foxes. But this is the tale of a cockerel who was cleverer still.

The cockerel belonged to the people of a big city and they thought the world of him, for he always gave them warning when the sun was going to rise. They would have overslept time and time again had it not been for the cockerel. They kept him in a special little house in a field, where they had kept his father before him. And not only his father, but his grandfather and his great grandfather and all his other direct ancestors for the family was as old as the city itself.

One day through the hedge that surrounded the field, came creeping a sly red fox. The cockerel hopped up on to a little mound to get out of the visitor's way but the fox sat down and began to talk to him, as soft as butter and as sweet as sugar.

"Admirable, handsome, bright-eyed, silver-tongued Mr Cockerel," said he. "I knew your father in days gone by. Ah! He was a wonderful old cockerel! I could tell you many a story of the things he did!"

The cockerel put his head on one side and blinked his bright eyes complacently.

"His voice, too!" went on Mr Fox. "Never was there such a musical voice! To hear him sing Cock-a-doodle-doo you would think that all the nightingales of the district were having a concert!"

He paused a moment, then said under his breath, "What would I not give to hear for myself if you have such a voice as your father!"

There was silence for a second. Then, Cock-a-doodle-doo-oo-oo" went the cockerel on the mound, his mouth wide open and his eyes tightly shut. "Cock-a-doodle-doodle-doodle-dud-dud-squawk!"

He choked shrilly over the last doodle and ended up with a terrible gurgling squawk. For the fox had leapt on to the mound, seized him in his mouth and was running away with him!

"Squawk! Squawk! Squawk!" screamed the cockerel again; so that the people in the city, hearing him, called to each other in dismay.

"Do you hear that? A fox is running away with our cockerel!"

But by this time the cockerel was pulling himself together for he was a very clever old cockerel. He stopped squawking and now it was his turn to talk as soft as butter and as sweet as sugar.

"My lord," he said to the fox, cunningly, "Do you know what the people of the city are saying? They are calling to each other that you are carrying off their cockerel! Was ever such a mistake made? It is to you I belong, my lord! I have never been the property of these people! You have always possessed me and naturally have at last come to claim your own. Open your lordly mouth, my lord, and tell the foolish people that I am yours!"

Mr Fox's jaws opened wide. He put his head over his shoulder and called out grandly to the people who were running after him: "This is my cockerel, good folks. He says so himself!"

Then he shut his mouth again as quickly as possible but there was no cockerel there now! As soon as Mr Fox had opened his jaws Mr Cockerel had flown out of them and perched himself, crowing triumphantly at the top of a tall tree.

"What lies you are telling!" cried the cockerel, quite forgetting the lies he had told himself. "I do not belong to you and never did! I belong to the people of the city and they will soon arrive at the foot of the tree and take me safely home in a bag!"

Sure enough, they did. And while Mr Cockerel was chuckling and crowing contentedly as he was carried home in the bag, Mr Fox was – what do you think Mr Fox was doing?

Well, he was hitting his own mouth hard against the ground, and scolding it at the same time. "You foolish mouth!"

he said, "Don't you know your own business? There is a time to talk, but there is also a time to eat! You spent your breath in words, when if you had had any sense, you would have spent it in swallowing the cockerel! Oh, silly mouth! I will teach you sense!"

And no doubt Mr Fox's silly mouth learnt the lesson and succeeded in future in doing the right thing at the right time. As for Mr Cockerel, he never forgot that to shut your eyes and crow when a fox is talking to you is certain to end in serious trouble.

THE HEN'S REVENGE
By Benjamin Rabier

Little Bob was always teasing someone. No one had any peace. He teased his Mum and Dad, he teased his brothers and sisters, and he teased the animals on the farm.

One day, however, there came a chance for someone else to tease Bob. He was looking about the yard for someone to play with, when he saw a chick perched on the edge of the dog's bowl.

It was pecking at the dog's dinner of soup and bread.

"Now's my chance!" thought Bob. He picked up a stick and crept behind the chick. Then suddenly he gave it a poke with the stick.

The poor little thing fell into the bowl of food. It struggled and tried to get out. At last Mrs Hen came running up to help. When she saw what Bob had done, she was very angry.

"I'll pay you back, my lad!" she clucked. And off she went to dry her chick in the sun.

Bob was now tired of teasing and sat down for a nap.

"Now we'll see who can tease people," said Mrs Hen. Very quietly she crept up to the sleeping boy and untied the laces of his boots. Then she moved off to a safe distance to see how her trick would work.

Bob opened his eyes and stretched himself. Then up he got. But he tripped over his long bootlaces, and fell right into the pig's dinner!

"Bob, you naughty boy!" called his mother from the house. "You shall have a smack for spoiling your clothes."

"And I'll give you a bite for spoiling my food," shouted the pig and chased the boy into the house.

But Mrs Hen smiled to herself and hid her chick under her wing.

THE PROUD COCKEREL

Master Julius was so proud that he threw out his crop and preened himself. Master Julius, the cockerel, was going to be a father! Father to dozens of downy little chicks, because all the hens in the roost were laying.

The nests were full of eggs. Julius was beside himself with joy and vanity. There was no doubt that the farmer's wife would be thrilled and would give him some extra titbits.

He could just see himself ruling over a host of little hens who, in turn would lay eggs. His descendants would fill the farmer's wallet when he went to sell the eggs in the village.

Julius was impatient to let his friends know what a clever father he was. He covered the countryside in all directions excitedly telling his news. Sometimes exaggerating, sometimes telling one or two lies to the other cockerels who listened to him. They were dumbfounded, and a little jealous of his luck. His comb turned scarlet and quivered like a jelly, his eyes sparkled and his feathers fluffed up; he really did look grand.

Soon, there was not one roost in the neighbourhood that did not know about Julius becoming a father. Everyone was as impatient as he was for the great day.

One morning the farmyard was in turmoil. Startled clucking and high-pitched chirping rose to a deafening din. The moment had come for the chicks to hatch out of their shells. Julius preferred to wait until it was all over before making his grand entrance in triumph. He wanted to wait until the mothers had calmed down and the children were asleep under their comforting wings.

After biding his time Julius got ready and smoothed his brilliant feathers one last time. He raised his spurs and like a conqueror entered the building.

Horror! Despair! Julius looked thunderstruck at his offspring. What had happened? He was distraught but those stupid hens hadn't noticed a thing!

Among a few little golden-yellow balls, which he recognised as his children, were some awful grey creatures with flat beaks and webbed feet. There were others with rickety legs and piercing squeaks. Julius took refuge at the bottom of the garden, while his friends all laughed.

He did not realise that the farmer's wife had slipped some duck eggs, some turkey eggs and some guinea-fowl eggs under the broody hens.

Julius won't boast any more.

MRS CLUCKY HEN AND THE
SPARROW-HAWK
By Benjamin Rabier

One fine day Mrs Clucky Hen took her chicks for a walk.

She led them into the yard where the farmer's wife had hung her sheet, which she had been washing, out on the line to dry. And there the sheet flapped and sang in the wind over Mrs Hen's head.

Just then a hungry sparrow-hawk flew over the house. "Quick! Quick!" shrieked the hen. "Come, children, under my wings." And she tucked them underneath her and sat down on the ground, hoping they would be safe. But the sparrow-hawk began to swoop down on her, saying to himself, "first I will take the hen, and then I will take the chicks."

But a little mouse saw the hen's danger. Quickly she ran on to the window-sill of the house, and nibbled the clothes-line till it broke and let the sheet fall on the hen, just as the sparrow-hawk swooped down.

"Well, that's very odd!" said the sparrow-hawk. "A moment ago there was a hen and twenty chicks here. Now there is nothing but a sheet!" And with an angry squawk he flew away.

Soon afterwards Mrs Hen walked out from under the sheet and said to herself, "What a clever hen I am! I have saved all my children from the hawk!" She had not the sense to know that it was the clever little mouse who had saved her.

PATCH AND THE CHICKS

On a farm up in Durham, there were six little chicks who were deserted by the mother hen as soon as they were hatched. So the farmer's wife put them in a basket and carried them into the cottage to keep them warm by the fire. There they were discovered by a rough coated terrier, named Patch, who was at that time very sad because her little puppy had just died, and she began to look after the chicks as if they were her own children. The little chicks also turned to her quite naturally for care and protection.

She used to treat them very gently and would sit and watch them feed with the greatest interest. She would curl herself up and then let them climb about her and go to sleep between her paws. Sometimes she did not seem to consider the floor comfortable enough for her adopted family and would jump onto a wooden bench which stood in the kitchen and then with her feet she would pat the cushions into a cosy bed and very carefully would take one chick after another in her mouth and place them on the softest part.

Soon the time came for the chicks to be sent out into the world. One day when Patch was out for a walk they were taken to the farmyard. When the poor little dog returned she was quite broken-hearted and ran whining about the cottage. Then, as if seized with a sudden thought she walked out of the door and in a very short time she reappeared, followed by her feathered family and again they took up residence in the cottage. Every morning Patch used to take them out for a walk, and it was a most amusing sight to see the little terrier followed by a procession of six stately chickens.

THE EASTER EGG HEN
By LaVere Andersen

Of all the hens in Farmer Smith's flock, only Molly Hen was worried – because she was the only hen who had heard Sue and Bobbie Smith say that Easter would soon be here and that they wanted coloured eggs for their Easter baskets.

Molly could see it was up to her to lay the coloured eggs.

But she didn't know how.

Try as she would, every egg she laid was white.

She went to Fido Dog for advice, although she felt foolish asking a dog how to lay an egg. Still Fido was an educated dog because once he had followed Sue and Bobbie to school and hidden under Bobbie's desk until the teacher found him and put him out. Fido said he had learned a lot in school that day.

When Molly told him how worried she was, he shook his head. "You can't help it that you're a country hen," he said.

"All the coloured eggs are laid by city hens and city hens are very smart."

"Is that so?" snapped Molly. "I guess I'm just as smart as they are! I'll lay a coloured egg if I have to stand on my head!"

"No, no!" said Fido hurriedly. "I don't think that's the way city hens do it."

"Then how?" demanded Molly, ruffling her feathers so indignantly that she quite overlooked a fat earthworm who wriggled out of the ground beside her. Willie Worm took one look at the angry hen and slid back into the safety of his tunnel.

"Well," said Fido, "at school the teacher talked about habits. Maybe you've sat on the same nest so long you've got into the habit of laying the same kind of eggs. Go and sit on some green grass and you'll lay a green egg."

Molly was delighted. She went hunting for green grass.

Most of the grass was still brown from winter, but she found a patch of young green blades in the shelter of the fence.

She sat on it. Then she cackled proudly that she had laid a green egg.

But when she got up and looked, the egg was white.

She went back to Fido.

"Never mind," he said. "I never cared for green, anyway. It's too common – green grass, green trees – why, they say even the moon is made of green cheese."

"Any colour," begged Molly. "I just don't want to disappoint the children."

Fido nodded. "At school the teacher said if a child eats a good breakfast he will have a good day. So it stands to reason if a hen eats a red breakfast she will have a red egg. Go and eat a red breakfast."

Molly clucked her thanks and went hunting for a red breakfast.

As she searched the garden path, she spied Willie Worm humping along, whistling cheerfully to himself. She would have loved to eat him, but he wasn't red enough. Willie nodded and humped along faster.

In the hayfield Molly found a red hair ribbon Sue had lost. She sat down by it to wait for breakfast time.

Next morning she ate the hair ribbon – although it was hard work. Then she cackled proudly that she had laid a red egg.

But when she looked, the egg was white.

In despair, she returned to Fido.

"Oh well," he shrugged, "red is too common anyway. Red roses, red fire trucks – why, even Rudolph the Reindeer has a red nose." He tapped his teeth thoughtfully with his paw nails. "At school the teacher said if you think hard enough that you can do a thing, you can do it. Go and think that you can lay a nice blue egg."

Molly sighed and sat down on the iris bed to think.

All night she sat there, staring at the velvety blue night sky and clucking softly to herself. "A country hen can lay a nice blue egg."

Dew dampened her feathers. Her neck grew stiff from craning upwards at the midnight blue sky. Her head began to ache. She got tired and cold and mixed up. Still she sat, hoarsely croaking, "A nice blue hen can lay a country egg."

At dawn, Willie Worm came humping past on his way home from an overnight hike. Molly would have enjoyed eating him, but her neck was too stiff to bend down. Willie waved in a friendly way.

At last Molly cackled proudly that she had laid a nice blue egg.

But when she looked, she knew she was a failure. It was the whitest egg she had ever laid.

Just as the Easter morning sun shone over the roof, Sue and Bobbie skipped from the house, laughing and looking under bushes and behind trees. Molly had the horrible thought that they might be looking for Sue's hair ribbon!

Then the children began to find eggs – coloured eggs! – hidden around the yard. They put the eggs into Easter baskets.

Then they went back into the house.

Sadly, Molly shuffled to the open kitchen door and peeked in.

Mrs Smith stood at the stove. She was saying, "What shall we do? Last night when we coloured the Easter eggs to hide, we forgot to save some eggs for breakfast!"

Sue saw Molly at the door. She cried, "Molly hasn't been on her nest lately. The other day I heard her cackling by the fence. Maybe she laid an egg there."

Bobbie said, "Yesterday I heard her in the hayfield."

Farmer Smith said, "This morning I heard her in the iris bed."

The children ran outside the house.

Soon they returned with three white eggs – Molly's eggs!

"This was the best egg hunt of all," said Sue. "Because I'm hungry and these eggs are to eat!"

"Yes," agreed Bobbie. "Coloured eggs are nice to play with but give me good old scrambled eggs any time."

"Thanks to Molly, we'll have a nice breakfast," said Mrs Smith.

Molly shuffled back to the barnyard, her head high.

"Forget coloured eggs," she told Fido importantly. "I can't waste my time on playthings. I am a breakfast-egg hen."

"Of course," said Fido. "Playthings are too common. Play toys, play clothes, play ring-a-ring-o'roses ..."

Just then Willie Worm came humping up. Molly wanted to eat him, but now it would be like eating somebody she knew. She didn't have the heart.

Willie bowed politely to her and said, "Good morning. I'm glad you've discovered you're a breakfast-egg hen."

"You mean you knew it all the time?" gasped Molly.

"Oh yes," said Willie. "And I know that Fido is a watchdog and town hens grow fat drumsticks and worms tempt fish to bite. Everybody has their own work to do."

"Why, you clever fellow!" beamed Molly. "I believe you're right!"

Willie squirmed in a pleased way. "Happy Easter!" he said.

"Happy Easter, everybody!" said Molly.

THE DOG AND THE COCKEREL
Traditional story from Russian Tales

Once upon a time a man, who had a dog and a cockerel, had no food to give them because his crops had failed. So the dog said to the cockerel, "Well brother Peter, I think we should get more food to eat if we went and lived in the forest than here at our master's, don't you?"

"Yes," said the cockerel, "Let's be off." So they said goodbye to their master and mistress and went off to see what they could find. And they went on and on but couldn't find a nice place to stop in. Then it began to grow dark and the cockerel said: "Let's spend the night in a tree. I'll fly up on to a branch and you get into the hole under the tree. We'll pass the night somehow."

So the cockerel made his way to a branch, tucked in his toes and went to sleep and the dog made himself a bed under the tree. And they slept all night; and in the morning, when it began to get light, the cockerel woke up and crowed as loudly as he could: "Cock-a-doodle-doo! Cock-a-doodle-doo! All wake up! All get up! The sun will soon be rising and the day will soon begin!"

And he crowed so loudly that a fox nearby heard him and said to himself, "What a funny thing for a cockerel to be crowing in the forest! He must have lost his way and can't get out again!"

And he began to look for the cockerel and after a bit he saw him sitting upon the branch of the tree. "Oho!" said the fox to himself, "He'll make a fine meal! How can I get him to come down from there?"

So he went up to the tree and said to the cockerel, "What a fine cockerel you are! I've never seen such a fine one in all my days! What lovely feathers, just as if they were covered with gold! And your tail! I can't tell you how fine it is! And what a sweet voice you've got! I could listen to it all day and all night. Do come a little nearer and let's get to know each other a little better. I've got a party on at my place today and I shall have lots of food and drink for you if you will come. Let's go along to my home."

"Very well," said the cockerel, "I'll come, only you must ask my friend too. We always go about together."

"And where is your friend?" asked the fox.

"Down below in the hole under the tree," said the cockerel. And the fox poked his head into the hole thinking there was another cockerel there, when the dog popped out his head and caught Mr Fox by the nose!

ELEVEN BLACK CHICKS AND HOW THEY GREW
By Clara Dillingham Pierson

When the Speckled Hen wanted to sit there was no use in trying to talk her out of the idea, for she was a very set hen. So the farmer's wife fixed her a fine nest and put thirteen eggs into it. They were Black Orpington eggs, but the Speckled Hen did not know that. The hens that had laid them could not bear to sit, so, unless some other hen did the work which they had left undone, there would have been no Black

Orpington chicks. This is always their way and people have grown used to it.

Still, the Black Orpington hens talk very reasonably about it. "We will lay plenty of eggs," they say, "but some of the common hens must hatch them." They do their share of the farmyard work – only they insist on choosing what that share shall be.

When the Speckled Hen came off the nest with eleven black chicks (two of the eggs did not hatch), she was not altogether happy. "I wanted them to be speckled," she said, "and not one of the whole brood is." That was why she grew so restless and discontented in her coop, although it was roomy and clean and plenty to eat and drink had been given to her. She was quite happy only when they were safely under her wings at night. And they always had such a time getting settled!

When the sunbeams came more and more slantingly through the trees, the chicks felt less and less like running around. Their tiny legs were tired and they liked to cuddle down on the grass in the shadow of the coop. Then the Speckled Hen often clucked to them to come in and rest but they liked it better in the open air. The Speckled Hen would also have liked to be out of the coop, yet the farmer kept her in. He knew what was best for hens with little chicks and also what was best for the tender young lettuces and radishes in his garden.

When the sun was nearly down, the Speckled Hen clucked her come-to-bed cluck which was quite different from her food cluck or her hawk cluck and the little black chicks ran between the bars and crawled under her feathers. The Speckled Hen began to look fatter and fatter and fatter. Sometimes one little fellow would scramble up on to her back and stand there while she turned her head from side to side, looking at him with first one and then the other of her round yellow eyes and scolding him all the time. It never did any good to scold, but she said she had to do something and with ten other children under her wings it would never do for her to stand up and tumble him off.

All the time that they were getting settled for the night the chicks were talking in sleepy little cheeps and now and then one of them would poke his head out between the feathers and tell the Speckled Hen that somebody was pushing him. Then she would be more puzzled than ever and cluck louder still. Sometimes, too the chicks would run out for another mouthful of chick crumbs or a few more drops of water.

There was one little fellow who always wanted something to drink just when he should have been going to sleep. The Speckled Hen used to say that it took longer for a mouthful of water to run down his throat than it would for her to drink the whole bowlful. Of course it did take quite a while, because he couldn't hurry it by swallowing. He had to drink as all birds do, by filling his beak with water and then holding it up until the last drop had trickled down into his stomach.

When the whole eleven were at last safely tucked away for the night, the Speckled Hen was tired but happy. "They are good children," she often said to herself, "even if they are Black Orpington. They might be just as mischievous if they were speckled; still, I do wish that those stylish-looking

Black Orpington hens would raise their own broods. I don't like to be foster-mother to other hens' chicks." Then she would slide her eyelids over her eyes and doze off and dream that they were all speckled like herself.

There came a day when the coop was raised and they were free to go where they chose. There was a fence around the vegetable garden now and netting around the flowerbeds but there were other lovely places for scratching up food, for nipping off tender young green things, for picking up the fine gravel which every chick needs, and for wallowing in the dust. Then the Black Orpington chicks met all the other hens. They were rather afraid of the Sussex Cockerel because he had such a gruff way of speaking and they liked the Dorkings, yet the ones they watched and admired and talked most about were the Black Orpington cockerel and hen.

There were many chickens on the farm who did not have family names and the Speckled Hen was one of these. They had been there longer than the rest and did not really like having new people come to live in the poultry yard. It was annoying, too when the older hens had to hatch the eggs laid by the newcomers.

It is said that this was what made the Speckled Hen leave the eleven little Black Orpington chicks after she had been out of the coop for a while. They had been very mischievous and disobedient one day and she walked off and left them to care for themselves while she started to raise a family of her own in a stolen nest under the straw-stack.

When night came, eleven little Black Orpington chicks did not know what to do. They went to look for their old coop, but that had been given to another hen and her family. They walked around looking very small and lonely and wished they had listened to the Speckled Hen and made her love them more. At last they found an old crate which reminded them of a coop and so seemed rather homelike. It stood, top down, upon the ground and they were too big to crawl through its barred sides, so they did the best they could and huddled together on top of it. If there had not been a stone-heap near, they could not have done that, for their wing feathers were not yet large enough to help them flutter. The bravest chick went first, picking his way from stone to stone until he reached the highest one, balancing himself awhile on that, stretching his neck towards the crate, looking at it as though he were about to jump and then seeming to change his mind and decide not to do so after all.

The chicks on the ground said he was afraid and he said he wasn't any more afraid than they were. Then, after a while he did jump – a strange, floppy, squawky kind of jump, but it landed him where he wanted to be. After that it was his turn to laugh at the others while they stood teetering uncertainly on the top stone. They were very lonely without the Speckled Hen and each chick wanted to be in the middle of the group so that he could have others to keep him warm on all sides.

Somebody laughed at the most mischievous chick and told him he could stand on the crate's back without being scolded and he pouted his bill and said: "Much fun that would be! All I cared about standing on the Speckled Hen's back was to make her scold."

They slept safely that night and only awakened when the cockerels crowed a little while after midnight. After that they slept until sunrise and when the Shanghais and Dorkings came down from the apple tree where they had been roosting the Black Orpington chicks stirred and cheeped and looked at their feathers to see how much they had grown during the night. Then they pushed and squabbled for their breakfast.

Every night they came back to sleep on the crate. At last they were able to spring up into their places without standing on the stone-pile and that was a great day. They talked about it long after they should have been asleep and were still chattering when the Sussex cockerel spoke: "If you Black Orpington chicks don't keep still and let us sleep," said he, "some owl or weasel will come for you and I shall be glad to have him!"

That frightened the chicks and they were very quiet. It made the Black Orpington hen uneasy though and she whispered to the Black Orpington cockerel and wouldn't let him sleep until he had promised to fight anybody who might try to carry one of the chicks away.

The next night, first one chick and then another kept tumbling off the crate. They lost their patience and said such things as these to each other: "You pushed me! You know you did!"

"Well he pushed me!"

"Didn't!"

"Did too!"

The Sussex cockerel became very cross because they made so much noise and even the Black Orpington cockerel lost his patience.

"You may be my children," he said, "but you do not take your manners from me. Is there no other place on this farm where you can sleep?"

"We want to sleep here," answered the chick on the ground. "There is plenty of room if those fellows wouldn't push." Then he flew up and clung and pushed until some other chick tumbled off.

"Well!" said the Black Orpington cockerel. And he would have said much more if the Black Orpington hen had not fluttered down from the apple tree to see what was the matter. When he saw the expression of her eyes he decided to go back to his perch.

"There is room," said the chicks, contradicting her. "We have always roosted on here."

"There is not room," said the Black Orpington hen once more. "How do your feathers grow?"

"Finely," they said.

"And your feet?"

"They are getting very big. Do you think the Speckled Hen could cover you all with her wings now?"

The chicks looked at each other and laughed. They thought it would take three speckled hens to cover them.

"But she used to," said the Black Orpington hen. She did not say anything more. She just looked at the crate and at them and at the crate again. Then she walked off.

After a while one of the chicks said: 'Perhaps there isn't room for us all there.'

The mischievous one said: "If you little chicks want to roost there, you may. I am too large for that sort of thing." Then he walked up the slanting board to the apple tree branch and perched there beside the young Sussexes. Before long his brothers and sisters came also and heard him saying to one of his new neighbours, "Oh, yes, I much prefer apple trees but when I was a chick I used to sleep on a crate."

"Just listen to him!" whispered the Black Orpington cockerel. "And he hasn't a tail-feather worth mentioning!"

"Never mind," answered the Black Orpington hen. "Let them play that they are grown up if they want to. They will be soon enough."

THE CLUCKING HEN
By A Hawkshawe

Pray will you take a walk with me,
My little wife, today?
There's barley in the barley fields,
And hay seeds in the hay.

Thank you, said the clucking hen,
I've something else to do.
I'm busy sitting on my eggs;
I cannot walk with you.

The clucking hen sat on her nest,
She made it in the hay;
And warm and snug beneath her breast,
A dozen white eggs lay.

Crack crack, went all the little eggs,
Cheep cheep the chickens small!
Cluck! Said the clucking hen,
Now I have you all.

Now come along, my little chicks
I'll take a walk with YOU.
Hello then crowed the barn-door
cockerel,
And cockadoodle doo.

THE WHITE HEN
By Christina Rossetti

A white hen sitting
On white eggs three;
Next, three speckled chickens
As plump as plump can be.

An owl and a hawk
And a bat come to see;
But chicks beneath their mother's wing
Squat safe as safe can be.

A LITTLE TALK
Anon

The big brown hen and Mrs Duck
Went walking out together;
They talked about all sorts of things
The farmyard and the weather.
But all I heard was: "Cluck, Cluck,
        Cluck!"
And "Quack, Quack Quack!"
        from Mrs Duck.